THE SOMALI
DECEPTION
EPISODE IV

DANIEL ARTHUR SMITH

The Somali Deception Episode IV
Copyright © 2010-14 Daniel Arthur Smith
All rights reserved Holt Smith ltd
Second Edition
Cover Design and Formatting by Daniel Arthur Smith
Edited by Crystal Watanabe

Published by Holt Smith Limited
ISBN: 0988649365
ISBN-13: 978-0-9886493-6-1

Also Written by Daniel Arthur Smith

The Cameron Kincaid Adventures
The Cathari Treasure
The Somali Deception

The Literary Fiction Series
The Potter's Daughter
Opening Day: A Short Story

The Horror Series
Agroland

~*~

For Susan, Tristan, & Oliver, as all things are.
&
To all of the others that choose to use crayons to color
their rainbows.

~*~

.

EPISODE IV

CHAPTER 57
GSTAAD, SWITZERLAND

The Volvo was travelling much faster than the posted limit, and as they traversed the incline of the winding road, Pepe continued to accelerate. The engine loaded RPMs onto each gear in succession, amplifying the illusion of speed and momentum. Cameron felt the sensation of being thrust up, out, and around the curves. He would have preferred to drive, yet had to defer to Pepe. Before leaving Paris, Pepe had secured the car, so there was never a question or an option for Cameron to do more than ease back and take in the Alps.

Of things to see in the world, the scenery of the Alps was among the most beautiful. A Mozart sonata filled the car. Cameron tapped his knee to the exhilarating tempo. The thinner air of the higher elevation gave the shimmering surface of Lake Geneva a fairy tale glisten. The iconic Alps, the pastoral valleys, and glacier groomed slopes were all postcard perfect. From the French Alps through the Swiss, the villages became evermore ornate. Even the jumbled architecture of Montreux, spanning from medieval snapshots of eras past to modern symbols of culture and the utmost wealth, had an enticing appeal.

Cameron and Pepe would soon arrive at their destination in the Bernese Oberland, a fairy tale in the Alps, brought to life by the architectural wonders of the Gstaad super rich. Each chalet was a paradise, an oasis, a manifestation of the vanity of artisans, architects, and interior designers with no budget limitation. The breathtaking uniform chalets, ornately carved from local wood, each hid a literal underground fortress with which Cameron was familiar. The picture perfect facades, a modest three meters above the surface, hid high-tech fortresses five times as large in the depths of Oberbort, Gstaad's most fashionable area. Reinforced by nuclear bomb proof concrete, these mansions under the earth held in their bellies swimming pools, fitness centers, spas, movie theaters, vintage car stocked garages, and wine cellars large enough to store a small vineyard. Cameron had been here several times before as a chef, and to play, and years ago as an agent. Quieter than St. Moritz and far more exclusive, the unscrupulous found comfort amongst celebrity and wealth.

Five minutes from the Gstaad Palace hotel, the valley's monument to prestige, Pepe found the driveway to the home of Demetrius Stratos. Demetrius' home, arguably the most expensive estate in Gstaad, audaciously boasted two massive chalets on the inclined field, two heads attached to a far larger beast below.

Pepe and Cameron were fresh, clean, and in surprisingly good spirits. The death of the Somali warlord Ibrahim Dada at Pepe's hand was an apparent catharsis. Though he had not yet found his sister Christine, taken from the hijacked yacht Kalinihta, Pepe was jubilant, almost his old jolly self. Pepe's mood in turn lightened Cameron's. The violence of the previous evening and the day before, of every day of the past week in Somalia, Dubai, London, and Paris, had become a perverse normal. The reinforced conditioning and training of his younger super commando self had overridden any morality play his mature psyche had applied to the events of the preceding days. Cameron was, after all, stoic by nature; that had been a key factor in his promotion to the Green Dragons. He accepted, believed, that the actions of the past could not be prevented or changed, only avenged, and that was what they were here in Gstaad to do. Avenge Pepe's sister, Cameron's former lover, Christine, for the wrongdoing at the hands of Nikos Stratos.

Neither Pepe nor Cameron had spoken of Alastair Main. Three days prior, their friend Alastair had been by their side. He had split off to piece together information that could help them in their search. That the two had not mentioned him did not mean their friend was absent from their thoughts. Alastair had a history with Nikos. To openly speak of their friend could lead down a path that neither wanted to walk.

Without words, Cameron and Pepe had made the mutual decision that they alone would deal with Nikos.

CHAPTER 58
GSTAAD, SWITZERLAND

Despite the prominent portion of Demetrius Stratos' estate being hidden below them, deep beneath the earth, what was above ground still gave the impression of grandeur. The first of the two mammoth wood faced chalets towered above them. The Greek shipping tycoon was obviously immune to the visible height limit imposed on the mere millionaires that peppered the mountainside around him. To their front was a garage door that Cameron calculated, by the dimensions, was the entrance not to the garage proper, rather to an auto elevator designed to transport the Stratos fleet of unique Ferraris and Lamborghinis to and from the depths below. Attached to the garage overlooking the valley was a building aligned in style with the two brethren above, yet miniature in size and status.

Cameron gazed out over the town of Gstaad in the valley below and then, momentarily unsure, asked Pepe, "Demetrius is expecting us?"

"He is expecting us," said Pepe.

"And he knew who you were?"

"I believe he knows who we are, he has been funding

our expedition. Anyway, I did not speak to him, I spoke to an assistant."

The heavy wooden door of the miniature chalet opened and from within stepped an exquisitely beautiful young woman. She wore tight fitting slacks and a wool sweater, predictable Alpen garb.

"This must be her," said Cameron.

The young woman said nothing. As the door pulled shut behind her, she looked fixedly at Pepe and Cameron. Her eyes appeared to pair with each of them. That her sultry gaze was at the same time obviously innocent yet seductive was provoking. She reminded Cameron of paintings he had seen, the Mona Lisa, or the Girl with a Pearl Earring, the way the women in the portraits poured out in a gaze, fixed on the observer, in silent communication. She offered them a pleasant smile, the knowing kind of smile that said, *Feel at home, you are welcome here.* Her light hair was full, blown out, and her relaxed nature implied a woman on holiday rather than an assistant to an industry mogul. Cameron pondered that she could easily have been a model, or an actress, and that perhaps at one time she had been.

The young woman's voice was full and confident, "Hello, you must be Mister Laroque and Mister Kincaid."

"Yes," said Pepe, he stepped toward the front of the Volvo to meet their greeter. "I am Pepe Laroque, and this is my colleague, Cameron Kincaid. Please call me Pepe, mademoiselle."

"And please, call me Cameron."

"Okay, Pepe, Cameron, I am Mister Stratos' assistant, Annalisa Droukos. Please call me Annalisa. Mister Stratos is expecting you, if you could follow me."

Annalisa offered another pert smile and then led them to an entrance set in the stacked boulders that composed the lower wall of the chalet. From a treetop to the left of the mammoth chalet came a sharp flash of light. Cameron met Pepe's eyes to see if he had noticed the sniper in the trees, obviously a member of the Stratos' security team. Pepe winked back and subtly nodded, shifting his brow in the direction to the eave above Cameron's shoulder. Cameron casually looked back over the valley and then forward again, catching the subtle red LED adjacent to the buttonhole camera that undoubtedly filled the screen of some internal security room deep in the belly of the estate. Though Annalisa did not wait for any signal or clearance, Cameron was sure he heard a faint click the second before she touched the handle of the door. If she had heard a lock releasing, she appeared not to notice, pulling the door open as casually as one goes from one room to the next.

The interior of the chalet was radically different from the fairy tale facade. The walls were rosewood paneled midway up to a small ledged molding, and then papered deeply red the remainder of the way up to an intricately carved wood ceiling. The indirect light cast the illuminating effect of oil lamps or candles, reminiscent of a train car or old Victorian manor. Along the crimson wall were photographs spaced every half meter. In an automated rehearsed fashion, Annalisa began to list off the people pictured by rote.

"On the wall you will find photos of some of the illustrious guests of the chalet as well as friends of the Stratos family. Pictured with Mister Stratos' father you will see Mister Churchill and in the next, you will see Mister Stratos himself, with the Queen, and in the next with Prince Charles and Princess Diana." Cameron recognized the Greek shipping mogul from the photo back at Alastair's cottage on the Laikipia plateau. Demetrius' well-groomed midnight hair was slicked back and below his chin; he wore a cravat, and on his finger, a wide gold ring with a red ruby setting. His hair, the cravat, and ring were consistent, no matter the age of the photo. Cameron had a brief imaginative flash of Demetrius as a small schoolboy with the same slick hair, silk cravat, and large gold ring.

As they continued through a maze of corridors and

stairwells, Annalisa continued describing the endless pictures and shelved artifacts. Along the way, they passed several dark lacquered doors that appeared, after a few hallways, confusingly the same; the same crystal knobs, the same order of sconces, and the portraits only subtly different than the last. Occasionally there would be an open room or a few open rooms together. Always the tour pressed on, focusing on the portrait collection of the world's elite. Initially, Cameron thought the tour a mere embellishment on the part of Demetrius, showing off the aristocrats, new and old, which were friends of the Stratos family. Then Cameron deduced the true purpose of the tour. The trivial information was meant to distract guests as they were led through the complex interior of the mansion.

After fifteen minutes of photos and trinkets, they came to a set of wooden double doors, black lacquered as the many before. Again Cameron heard a faint click before Annalisa reached for the lead crystal knob.

"This is Mister Stratos' library," she said. "Please wait here and he will join you shortly."

The Stratos library, in the same manner as every other part of the chalet they had been shown, resembled a museum. The walls of the large library were entirely covered, with the exception the wall bordering the door. The wall was rosewood paneled midway and topped with the same crimson that papered the hallway. On either side of the door were recently stocked sidebars, one with assorted cheeses and meats, and the other with decanters and a crystal bowl of ice.

The ceiling was a continuation of exaggerated ornate woodcarvings, including two wooden cherubs at the base of a high backlit stained glass dome in the center. The sidewalls were shelved, floor to ceiling, with dark hued leather bindings, bright with accents of pressed gold and silver letters. On one shelf was a solitary device to detect moisture, and in another section, backlit behind glass, were ancient and rare tomes. The entirety of the back wall was also an exhibit behind glass. Covering the back wall from one side to another was an array of modern and ancient weapons. On the right side, a glass door shielded a recessed anteroom, the size of a large closet, lined with handguns of every age and make. The rest of the wall was adorned with antique edge weapons. Neatly displayed were row after row of swords, scimitars, spears, knives, and daggers. In the center of the room was a low table display case housing aboriginal blowguns, each surrounded by various feathered darts. Around the low table were four heavily cushioned dark leather chairs, and another four sat on the outer edge of the room, one in each corner.

The room was magnificent.

"You can help yourself with a drink from the sidebar," said Annalisa. "Is there anything special I can have brought in for you?"

Cameron raised his brow. "I believe we're fine, Annalisa."

"Excellent," said Annalisa. She gestured to an intercom near the door. "Just tap that button if you need anything. Mister Stratos will be with you shortly." She put a finger to her ear revealing a small emerald that mirrored the glint in her eyes. An earpiece. She smiled and then tilted her head toward the wall, fixed intently on a conversation that Cameron and Pepe were not privy to. Then Annalisa nodded her head, removed her finger, and returned her attention to the two men. "He is still on a call, so please make yourself comfortable."

"Thank you," the two said in near unison.

"And Mister Kincaid, um, Cameron," said Annalisa.

"Yes?"

"I enjoy your shows."

Cameron near winced. Though he had received many unexpected compliments that had caught him off guard, Annalisa's was different. He had begun to forget about his celebrity chef persona.

"Thank you for watching, I am glad you enjoy the

shows."

Annalisa's gaze appeared more intense, more eager to please, "As I said, if you need anything." Her last word hung in the air as she left them alone in the library.

Cameron shifted his eyes to Pepe. "Don't start."

"Dragon Chef," said Pepe haughtily. He winked at Cameron.

Neither took the offered drink, rather they both went to inspect the weapons display at the back of the library. Though Cameron and Pepe were not exactly weapons enthusiasts, they certainly had a predilection. Cameron's curiosity drew him toward the gun closet. Pepe, by no surprise to Cameron, was instinctively drawn to the edge weapons. The handguns in the recessed display case were no doubt some of the rarest, and those that were more common, Cameron surmised, had a special property or past. Cameron imaged a man of Demetrius' wealth would have the gun that killed Hitler if that device was obtainable.

"Cameron," said Pepe, his voice low. "Come here for a moment. I want you to see this."

Cameron joined Pepe, scanning the iron and steel as he passed the wall. "What did you find?"

"You are not going to believe this," said Pepe.

In the case in front of Pepe, a series of fifty daggers were pinned to the red velvet wall, in two rows of twenty-five. The daggers appeared to be arranged by age. Some of the daggers were very ornate, others mere missiles, all of them with the same Latin inscription, 'Caedite eos! Novit enim Dominus qui sunt eius.'

Cameron translated the familiar phrase, "Kill them all. Surely the Lord discerns which ones are his."

"Can you believe he has these?" asked Pepe.

"Well, he is a collector, and we have a few of our own."

"You think they belonged to the agents of the same clandestine group we met up with?" asked Pepe. "Some of these are very old."

"If you would have asked me before Quebec, I might have said something different. Marie said the Rex Mundi has many agents, knowing and not knowing. Who knows how far back in history the cells go. Marie said they went back to the beginning."

"The beginning of what?" asked Pepe.

From the door of the library came a deep voice, "To the beginning of the world."

The two spun to see Demetrius Stratos enter the room. Stratos lifted a finger in the direction of the case. "You find the daggers interesting?"

CHAPTER 59
GSTAAD, SWITZERLAND

Well-tanned and debonair, Demetrius Stratos could have been posing for a portrait. Framed between the library doors, the crimson at his back exaggerated the brilliance of his pressed white shirt, and, as in every photo, his dark hair was slicked back, around his neck he wore a silk cravat, and the gold ruby ring, as crimson as the backdrop, was on his hand. Stratos' blue eyes penetrated the room. The kind look on his face did not disguise the fact that he was intensely and steadily assessing his two visitors.

Having previously met a number of people associated with wealth or celebrity, Cameron was not put off by the man's scrutiny. The pause was becoming slightly uncomfortable when Cameron realized Stratos was exercising a familiar technique. The confident gaze was to give the impression that Stratos could judiciously size up a man. Cameron and Pepe were to understand him to be serious and reliable, or that Stratos had tallied their flaws. Cameron deduced that the magnate probably thought the two men had come to Gstaad for an additional fee for saving his son Nikos from the coastal pirates. The correct soldier's response was to mirror Stratos with a stern gaze to set him at ease. A stare that would instill in the rich man the impression that Cameron and Pepe were not mere fortune hunters. So Cameron and Pepe returned the stare.

"Those daggers are a very rare find," said Stratos, before either Cameron or Pepe spoke. He crossed the room to join Cameron and Pepe near the glass-covered wall.

Pepe began to speak, "Mister—"

Raising a quick hand, Stratos cut Pepe off, "Yes, yes, we can forego the formality of introductions. You know who I am, I know who you are. Now let me tell you about these daggers you are admiring." From his pocket, Stratos pulled a small fob, similar to one used as a car key. He subtly tapped a button with his thumb and the glass began to slide to the side, disappearing into the end of the shelved wall. When the glass cleared the fifty daggers, Stratos removed one from the section that appeared among the oldest. Stratos chose one of the few with a hilt, a white hilt. "These daggers are very rare finds," said Stratos. He held the dagger to demonstrate the peculiarities. "Take this specimen for example. Fine metallurgy, a perfect balance, and the hilt—"

"Made of bone, correct?" asked Pepe.

"Yes," said Stratos, pleased by Pepe's assessment. He held the dagger by the blade between his knuckles and thumb so that the hilt was fully revealed. "In fact this hilt is made of bone, as are a few others. Some collectors have asserted the bone is from a large mammal, a cow or a horse, others say a predator. They are wrong, of course. I had a DNA test performed, not on this blade alone but the other bone handled daggers in this collection as well. You know what I found?"

"They are all human," said Pepe.

"That is correct." Stratos handed the blade to Pepe. "Each one, including the one you are holding, proved to be human bone. European, as a matter of detail."

Pepe inspected the dagger, twisting the blade from one side to the other. "For an older knife, this has fine craftsmanship."

"I agree. The articulate manner of the metal craft around the top and bottom of the hilt and the delicate inscription along the blade, all of the daggers share this. That is what ties the collection together, yet the style of lettering on this dagger... Well, the intricacy is unique."

"'Caedite eos! Novit enim Dominus qui sunt eius,'" said Cameron. "Kill them all. Surely the Lord discerns which ones are his."

"That is right, Mister Kincaid. Your Latin and vision are both spectacular. I find the inscriptions difficult to read in this light."

"We've actually come across these before," said Cameron.

Stratos peered into Cameron's eyes, his expression knowing, "So I've been told."

Cameron's throat slightly tensed. With his best face, he pretended not to have been surprised by the statement. Besides, Stratos must have heard him wrong. Stratos could not possibly guess that Cameron and Pepe once had such daggers in their possession. Stratos could not possibly be aware of how the daggers, worn by the Rex Mundi operatives, came into their possession—by the death of Rex Mundi agents. Perhaps Stratos was aware of the terrorist cult. Maybe Stratos was quite comfortable knowing that these instruments of death were all tokens of a cult. A cult, Cameron and Pepe realized, that went back hundreds of years, as dear Marie had told them before she died.

Stratos did not let the conversation pause. Cunningly, he changed the subject so as not to linger on his statement. "Well," he took the dagger back from Pepe to place back into the special reserved space in the collection. "I do want to welcome you. I want to thank you for saving my son, and insist you share a drink with me in thanks." Stratos turned toward the sidebar across the room. "I of course want to offer my condolences for your sister, Pepe. Dreadful, these animals." He spun around to face them, approaching the bar blindly. "And I do mean animals. I could not begin to tell you the trouble I have had with them in the past." At the bar, he again turned his back to them and began preparing three rock glasses of scotch. "Hijacking, hostages, the disregard for life and property. I understand the two of you have been pursuing her whereabouts." He spun back around, a scotch glass in each hand for the two men. "Here, have a seat."

"You should sit with us," said Cameron.

"Certainly, I intend to."

"Um, that is not what I meant. You see, we have found Christine, or at least finally know where to find her."

"That's fabulous," said Stratos. "We should be toasting." Cameron and Pepe each took a seat on the cushioned leather chairs in the center of the room. Stratos joined them.

"You might not think so in a moment," said Pepe.

"I don't understand."

"You will," said Pepe. He placed the small digital recorder on the display case table between them.

"You see," said Cameron. "We spoke with Abbo and Dada about your relationship with them."

Stratos' brow dropped.

"And we don't really care about that. But there is something else Dada shared with us. Well, you should hear this yourself. Pepe, if you please."

Pepe placed his index finger on the top of the recording device and pressed play.

CHAPTER 60
GSTAAD, SWITZERLAND

After listening to the torture of Ibrahim Dada and the coerced warlord's account of the hijacking of the Kalinihta, subsequent kidnapping, and the claim that responsibility fell on Nikos Stratos, Demetrius Stratos straightened in his chair. He ran his finger around the rim of his scotch glass, sipped, and then relished the alcohol for a moment.

Cameron sensed the cognitive dissonance plainly on Stratos. The inconsistent beliefs in the deceitful spoiled playboy Stratos knew his son to be conflicted with his implicit faith the boy would never be disloyal to his father. Cameron could not fault Stratos for believing the best of his only son. Every parent should be on the side of their child.

"That man would have said anything," said Stratos, affirming the reaction Cameron had predicted.

"You know who the man was on the recording," said Cameron. "You know Ibrahim Dada."

"Of course. I know that man is a scoundrel and despite his title as admiral or general or his diplomatic status. He is not much more than a common thug."

"We know of your dealings with Abbo, and we know Dada was trying to work with you."

Stratos raised his hands. "So you know. Business on the high seas is very complex. Since you have obviously come into some information I will tell you that many men do business with these and other unsavory people, small things, unavoidable, necessary evils." His face shrugged. "You have to imagine I run, not one, but rather several fleets of tankers and commodities." Stratos leaned in to the display case between them, resting his elbows on his knees. He set his rock glass on the table and then clasped his hands together. "That is why I find this impossible to believe. The idea my son would stage his own kidnapping in a plot to undermine me, a ridiculous notion. My son is many things, conniving and clever, yes. Disloyal he is not."

"Believe what you will," said Pepe. "We conducted more than one, shall we say, intense interviews. I do not believe these men were wanting to lie."

Stratos smirked at Pepe, "Interviews? A more precise description would be interrogations. Everyone knows tortured men will say anything. Dada was in fear of his life, and rightfully so if I understand correctly, and Abbo, what you did to him, really." Demetrius shook his head. "The local papers reported a high altitude gas accident. Don't forget I financed your endeavor. I know you two were behind the whole thing. Blowing him out the window of the Burj Khalifa." Stratos shook his head again. "That was unnecessary. Abbo was a lecherous, greedy man, yet he did business wisely. He kept his people reigned in and he was good for his word."

"I am sure Abbo was a great man," said Cameron.

Stratos appeared disgusted. He spoke coolly, "I am only saying that Abbo was not merely a thief," he flashed his eyes between them, "or a pirate. He knew how to do business in a way that was mutually beneficial to all persons."

"You call what you do there business?" asked Pepe.

Stratos rolled his eyes. "Business of a sort. I thought you were here to discuss something else."

"We are," said Cameron sensing the blood rising between Pepe and Stratos. "We do not wish to offend. We believe Nikos can help us to find Christine."

In contemplation Stratos wrapped his knuckles against the top of the display case glass in slow repetition, pausing between each tap. Then after a long pause, he congenially spoke again. "I will indulge you because you saved my son, and I understand your concern for the missing girl. Annalisa tells me that when Nikos left Lamu he went directly to Monaco, then sailed our yacht down to Ibiza. Apparently, he plans to stay at our Ibiza estate to do some sailing and clear his head. I will fly the two of you down there to confront Nikos. Then we can settle this once and for all."

"Ibiza, you say?" asked Pepe.

"Annalisa will have my jet prepped. I have a few things to tend to. Someone will be along to sort you so you can freshen up and we will leave in—" Stratos put his finger to his ear as Annalisa had earlier. "Yes, we can leave within the hour. I will meet you at the chopper."

CHAPTER 61
PARIS, FIFTEEN YEARS BEFORE

The bathroom floor was covered with layers of newspaper. Cameron had cleared one of little Moby's messes earlier and already there was another pool in the corner. Christine sat on the edge of the bed gazing down at the small brown ball frolicking at her feet. "He is so cute," she said, "this petit doggy."

Ten million years of evolution coursed through Cameron. He had made Christine happy and countless sparking endorphins issued his biological reward with a sense of elation, a euphoric well-being. The wine and chocolate did not hurt either. In his hand, he held the last of the wine, a half bottle of vin rouge pulled from the top of their short refrigerator. In his other hand, two small fruit glasses were pinched between his fingers. Cameron winked at Christine, put the bottle to his mouth, pulled the cork with his teeth, and then with a huff sent the plug flying across the room.

Christine giggled. She spoke softly, seduction in her eyes, "So gallant."

Cameron filled the two small glasses with a single pour and then offered one to Christine. "I aim to please, mademoiselle."

"Merci, monsieur," said Christine. She sipped, then stopped, overtaken by another giggle.

Cameron leaned forward to give Christine a quick peck. When he placed his mouth upon hers, she hooked an arm around his neck and squeezed, lifting herself from the bed to pull him down. Caught in the embrace, Cameron's balance wavered and he began to sink forward. The further he leaned the more passionately she kissed, melting into him, drawing him to the mattress. Awkwardly contorted, he continued to kiss her until he could lean no further without spilling wine. He shifted his foot to correct himself and lowered her gently back onto the bed, extending his arm up and away to balance the glass in his hand.

Free of her weight, Cameron unlocked the kiss and rubbed his nose against Christine's. "Careful, unless you want a wine shower."

"Would that be so bad?"

Cameron scrunched up one side of his face. "Maybe white wine would be better."

Christine set her glass of wine down on the bedside table, raised her arms up to embrace an invisible shower, and exclaimed, "Bathe me in a shower of champagne?"

"You would like that, would you?"

"Oui," said Christine, her voice cute. "Then you can clean me." She lifted her arms open to him. Cameron had another sip of his wine, set the glass near Christine's, and then settled into her embrace, this time falling with her onto the mattress. She touched her lips softly to his, her mouth open, not a full kiss, a precursor, a tease of what was to come next. She pulled slightly away and then kissed him again, this time with more intensity, more passion, and then the two rolled on their backs. They gazed up at what could have been a field of stars yet was merely plaster, dinged in spots, and yellowed in others. Cameron raised his forearm and Christine coiled hers so that the palms of their hands met and their fingers could clasp. This happened so naturally, in unison, their bodies and minds synchronizing.

Christine's voice was musically dreamy, "Today was perfect. I want you to be with me always."

"That would be nice," said Cameron. He wanted to be calm, truthful, and not let the reality of the short time they had together slip from him. Moments such as these, he thought Christine had tossed reality away, and that concerned him. Not in the sense he thought her irrational, rather he did not want to see her hurt.

Christine continued, "You could stop with the Legion, and then you could come to Paris, to always be here to look after me."

"One day I will," he said. "You know I am under contract."

Christine sighed. "Oui," she said. She rolled onto her side and brought her free arm around to run her fingers across his chest. She continued to softly rake him for a long moment and then, with a tint of intrigue asked him a question.

"Cameron?"

"Yes, Christine?"

"What if something were to happen to me?"

Cameron tilted his head toward hers. "What do you mean, something happen to you?"

Christine raised her brow. She had not actually thought of any one particular thing. "I don't know. What if somebody tried to hurt me, take me away in a grand kidnapping?"

"No one is going to kidnap you."

"What if somebody did? What if they try to steal me and you are not here to protect me? What if you are across the sea with my brother on some mission, doing who knows what?"

Cameron rolled to face Christine. "I promise. If anyone ever tries to take you, I will come to your rescue."

"You promise? You will be mon chevalier?"

"I promise, on my honor," said Cameron, and then he

kissed Christine again, harder than before, embracing her until their passions were satisfied.

CHAPTER 62
IBIZA

The group enjoyed a four-course dinner aboard Stratos' private jet. The meal consisted of salad, fresh Maine lobster, Wagyu steak, and black currant custard, and lasted the flight from Gstaad to Ibiza. No sooner had the dessert plates been collected than the jet prepared to touch down at the Ibiza airport, where two four-door Aston Martin Rapides were waiting. Stratos and his assistant Annalisa drove one, Cameron and Pepe the second. Because of his familiarity with the island, Cameron drove.

Cameron's past visits to Ibiza had not been as a chef. His time on the island had been spent as an agent of the Legion, posing as a civilian. His missions were of the same nature as those in Gstaad. Though not as exclusive as the Swiss enclave, Ibiza was simply another playground for celebrity, wealth, and the unscrupulous.

Tiers of holiday villas appeared to pop out of the ocean side hills surrounding the town of Ibiza, in the same fashion as the chalets that filled the mountainsides of the Bernese Oberland. On Ibiza, the facades peering down to the sea were all glass rather than carved wood, yet they created the same illusion of multi-dwellings peppering the island heights. The glass facades, the same as the wooden, were actually multi-levels of single homes, stealthily attached within the sparse forest and hillside. Hidden as well from the beautiful bay below were the sun decks, infinity pools, and the rear garages that housed high-end sports cars of all makes.

The wealthy occupants residing in the hills far above the crystal blue ocean, predominantly young foreigners, collectively slept until noon, napped late in the day, and then clubbed all night, making the sunrise their second sunset, what those of their ilk tagged as a 'disco sunrise'. The authorities' highly tolerant, blasé attitude toward the illicit behavior of the hill dwellers and Ibiza hippie kids that slept on the beach had earned the small Spanish island the well-deserved moniker, the 'Gomorrah of the Med.'

With the huge help of Annalisa's congenial demeanor and feminine wilds, Stratos had worked to calm the intentions of Cameron and Pepe. Requisitioning them a car from his fleet was part of the effort to build trust. Stratos had Annalisa call the staff ahead of the group's arrival to determine if Nikos was at the compound. Apparently, he was not. So when Cameron drove the Aston Martin into the parking bay, their expectation was that Nikos was already out for the evening. The playboy was surely at a café, preparing to watch the sunset, and would soon be partaking one of the islands famed mega-clubs. Nikos' absence suited Cameron fine. Without games or confrontation, the search for Christine would be easier.

The Stratos Ibiza compound was architecturally similar to the chalet in Gstaad, but at a smaller scale. When Annalisa led Cameron and Pepe into the principal dwelling, the main difference from the Gstaad decor was that the walls were ivory as opposed to the crimson paper they had seen during their small tour of the chalet. The walls were lined with photographs, as the chalet had been, however there were no signs of the antiqued Victorian motif. The décor of the Ibiza villa was youthful, modern, and tropical.

The central room opened to a high ceiling and the rooms of the next level shared the glass walled cerulean blue ocean view from the interior balcony. A tall bright tapestry hung on one side of the room and a large Britto multicolored pop canvas spanned the height of the other. Large fronds shot out of planters near the edge of the room and large puffy brilliant colored pillows covered the three white sofas and floor.

"Feel free to check every part of the house," said Stratos. "Annalisa has shut down security and will open any door that remains locked. I want this to be settled once and for all."

Cameron detected the temper of the Greek man was sneaking in. He deduced that Stratos was sure the villa was empty. Stratos certainly would have had Annalisa ask the staff. "We'll be quick," said Cameron, and to keep Stratos' temper from flaring added, "We appreciate the indulgence."

Already walking toward the white bar on the side of the room, his lip curled, his head nodding, Stratos turned his head back toward the two men. Precisely at that moment, Annalisa entered the room from behind them. She had excused herself to 'freshen up' on their arrival, and had changed into a revealing full bikini top with a flowing white wrap around her waist. When Cameron had first met her at the chalet he had been taken by her stunning beauty, yet her well-endowed proportions had been hidden beneath the slacks and wool sweater.

Annalisa raised her hand toward the staircase as if she were a hostess greeting the two men at a spa resort. "Gentlemen, if you can please follow me, we can begin the tour."

Annalisa had called it a tour, and her description could not have been more precise. The two followed her through every luxurious upstairs room, each with fine furnishings and an oceanic view. They followed through the glass walled suites to the sides of the central room, each with hot tubs and other amenities. Along her tour, Annalisa described the photos on the walls of the hallway and the special aspects of each room, as she had done at the chalet. They returned to the lower level and then toured every room there, and then went through a subterranean passage to the other villas. They toured the fully industrial kitchen equipped to cater hundreds, the large courtyard containing two infinity pools and three spa bathhouses, and then the staff villa, with a private pool and bathhouse that alone could compete with any resort.

For Cameron and Pepe's satisfaction, Annalisa took the time to openly speak with each staff member they came across. For each maid and gardener, she made an introduction and asked if they had seen Mister Nikos and when they each replied yes with an overly warm, pleasing smile that barely masked their individual disgust for the young master, she would ask if he had brought any guest to the villa, to which each of them replied no, or they did not know, or referred another staff member better fitted for ratting out the boss.

When they reached the wine cellar, Annalisa excused herself to get a key from the chef, explaining, "Some of the staff cannot resist temptation."

Alone, Pepe muttered to Cameron, "She knows we are not going to find a sign of Christine here."

Cameron whispered back, careful not to move his lips, due to the camera he was sure had them in focus. "I came to that conclusion the moment we arrived."

"They are nervous, though," said Pepe.

"Yeah, something is up. She may not be here at the villa, yet they certainly don't trust Nikos."

"I picked up on that as well."

Christine, of course, was not in the wine cellar, nor was she in the tree hidden security barracks, the movie theater, on the tennis court, or lastly, in the private rooms of Nikos and his father. These rooms were true examples of the extreme wealth of the Stratos clan. Annalisa was insistent that to visit the inner sanctum of Demetrius Stratos was a privilege granted to very few. Cameron imagined that to be true. There were plenty of other rooms to entertain any trysts the older bachelor may decide to partake, where the voluptuous Annalisa could assist him in other entertaining matters besides business. The study alone, the only darkened room in the compound, showed signs of wealth in every deep detail, from the soft leather paneled walls to the rare Brazilian hardwood desk.

Yet in all of these rooms there was no sign of Pepe's sister. Not even in Nikos' private wing. Cameron and Pepe were a bit perturbed for being granted access to the rooms of highest suspicion last. Granted, as Annalisa led them through each immaculate room, they saw no signs of foul play. Neither of the two suspected any evidence had been hidden or washed away as they were being distracted with a tour of the rest of the compound. These were the last rooms to visit because they were not on the tour map, not part of Annalisa's rote breakdown of each room and element.

Nikos' study is where they found their single clue. Much much simpler than his father's, the study's walls had the same ivory white as every other room, the desk a small wooden table, the shelves vacant of any collection of books. Of interest, though, was the picture-covered wall. Like his father and grandfather's thousand photos covering every bit of hall space in the chalet and villa, and most likely every other estate and home the family owned, these photos were of Nikos with an assortment of people. Yet the people pictured in these photos were no dignitaries or titans of business, all of these pictures were of Nikos and his friends. There was a picture that they had seen before, the one with Alastair by his side; a small brass tab on the frame said 'Kenya.' What drew Cameron and Pepe's interest was another photo. A picture of Nikos and another man, arm in arm, a half naked woman held by the waist on either side, surrounded by the colorful party array of a rave. Etched in the small brass plaque tacked to that frame were the words

'Ibiza, Stratosphere.'

Cameron and Pepe looked at each other knowingly. The Stratosphere was a club of repute where famous deejays flew in to host regular parties. The name had not clicked before.

Pepe tapped the bottom of the picture. "This is a great picture. Where was this taken?"

"Oh, that is Stratosphere, a fabulous club that Nikos co-owns. Very fun, you should try to visit—" she caught herself and stopped.

Pepe appeared jovial, "Stratosphere, a great name for a club. A nice play on words." He lifted his hands, molding some invisible clay. "A nice play on names." Then his tone shifted, "Is that where Nikos will be tonight?"

Annalisa's jaw tightened and her head shifted to the side to help fortify her resolve. She obviously realized she had said too much and that there was no backing away.

This was the time for Cameron to turn on his charm. He smiled subtly, and then with a low confident tone he asked Annalisa, "This club, Stratosphere, we are going to find him there, aren't we?"

Annalisa's eye darted from one side to another, searching for anyone that may be watching, or perhaps come to save her from betraying her employers. Then with obvious reluctance, she matched her eyes to Pepe and then to Cameron, and nodded her head, an affirmative yes.

CHAPTER 63
IBIZA

The taillights of the Aston Martin Rapide in front of them glowed unevenly against the late tangerine sky.

"Your boss doesn't know one of the LEDs is out on the right side," said Cameron. "I bet he won't be pleased."

Annalisa sighed, "I'll have the garage fix the light in the morning."

Pepe shuffled uncomfortably in the backseat. "How much farther do we have?"

"The club is off the main road between Ibiza Town and San Antonio," said Annalisa, "in walking distance to San Rafael."

"Near Amnesia?" asked Cameron. Cameron had one hand on the wheel and the other arm resting on the open window. The warm air of the island breezed into the car and washed over them.

"Stratosphere is between Amnesia and Privilege, Ibiza's other two famous nightclubs," said Annalisa. A subtle undertone to her voice told Cameron that Annalisa was still tense. Cameron had sized up Annalisa. She had not meant to lead them to Nikos, that was obvious, and the slip had her deeply concerned. Cameron also understood that

describing the world around her comforted the beautiful
Annalisa. He had met many people before that relished in
dissociative context. Stratos had given Pepe and Cameron
access to Annalisa and if Cameron wanted to turn her to his
advantage he first needed to calm her. To get her talking
before they reached the club. The club excited Annalisa and
she'd lowered her guard. She had mentioned Stratosphere
and then had she slipped. Stratosphere was a perfect topic
for discussion. "Stratosphere is pretty famous," said
Cameron. "I never put the two together, Stratos,
Stratosphere. I can't say I'm surprised, yet I'm curious.
How did Nikos end up with his own club?"

Cameron had been correct. He glanced into the
rearview and caught a wink from Pepe. Annalisa's eyes lit
up. "Stratosphere is one of the top three nightclubs on the
island. My favorite, then again maybe I'm partial, and the
story is a testament to Nikos."

"How's that?" asked Cameron.

"Like his father, if Nikos wants something he finds a
way."

"And he wanted a club? That does not sound like such
a challenge for the son of a billionaire."

"That's not what Nikos wanted. Since the sixties, the
large discothèques of Ibiza flourished as the destination
clubs of the Mediterranean. When disco died, techno music
took the Mediterranean and the rest of Europe in a wave
that would not catch on in the United States for almost
another twenty years. The eclectic blend of deejay-led dance
music, Balearic house, emerged as the new sound of Ibiza.
The mega nightclubs evolved with new names and images
for a new clientele, and Nikos Stratos was ripe for the birth
of the ecstasy filled rave scene."

"Right," said Cameron. Annalisa had gone into rote
brochure mode. "He was a rich playboy even then. I bet he
wanted to be a deejay."

"That's right," said Annalisa. He was fascinated with
techno. He owned a Roland TR-909 drum machine, and an

array of top of the line electronics and turntables to create his own music. He even hosted a couple of nights."

"I get it. Daddy would not let him be a musician. Let me guess, did he threaten to cut off the piggy bank?"

"Not quite, we are Greek, we indulge our children. His father did, of course, frown on the idea of Nikos being a deejay, so they came to an agreement his father would condone. Nikos picked up a premiere nightclub. The venue had been a successful discothèque back to the early seventies, yet had not made the transformation. Then he renamed the place Stratosphere. Like Privilege, the world's largest nightclub, the dance floor is the size of an aircraft hangar with a twenty-five meter high roof. There is also a splendid open-air back patio with a fountain between two swimming pools."

Cameron saw Pepe roll his eyes at Annalisa's rote tour description.

"Sounds more like a testament to Demetrius," said Cameron. "He convinced his son to give up his dream in exchange for a nightclub."

"Just the opposite," said Annalisa. "Nikos convinced his father to let him continue to pursue his hobby and develop the club. The club is successful, and so is Nikos. He has a regular night there as well as nights in London and Vegas."

"I don't keep up with the scene. Still, I don't believe I have ever heard of Deejay Nikos."

"That's because he uses an alias to deejay and wears a costume," said Annalisa. "You must have heard of Deejay Roboto."

Pepe leaned forward, "No, really? He is famous."

"I told you. Like his father and his father before him, Nikos always has what he wants."

CHAPTER 64
STRATOSPHERE, IBIZA

When the Aston Martins reached the Stratosphere nightclub, the last remnants of fuchsia lined the western sky. A large crowd of excited clubgoers hovered outside the main doors. Cameron could hear and feel the deep base thump of the trance music playing inside. Stratos led Cameron to the VIP entrance around the side of the building. A team of valets in tight black t-shirts sprinted to the doors of both cars. When Stratos and Annalisa exited the Aston Martins, two muscular security guards at the door sporting the same tight black tees as the valets snapped to attention and unclipped the velvet rope that gated the entrance. Annalisa was stunning. She wore the wrap she had changed into at the villa with the addition of a sheer white blouse to cover the bikini. Stratos had provided Cameron and Pepe with lighter attire appropriate for the warmer Ibiza evening and the sure to be stifling club interior. Stratos himself wore white linen slacks and shirt and, of course, a thin cravat tied tightly around his neck.

Cameron was beginning to wonder what Stratos was hiding beneath the silk necktie.

Through the threshold, the electronic rhythm of the

dance music washed over the group. The soup of pulsing digital notes thickened, tactile as mist or fog. Flashing multicolor lights synched to the sound system added a physical quality to the electronic tones. The effect was compulsory autonomic acceleration of the heart and lungs. Cameron's nervous system heightened, high on contact with the interior rave dimension. He glanced at Pepe and the two shared a knowing glint.

The private entryway was a velvet-curtained foyer. The main dance floor split out to the right, and to the left, a set of stairs was ghostly shadowed by the bright blinking lights in the cavern above. Stratos led the group the route of the stairs. The first landing of the staircase opened up to a suspended catwalk that stretched along the length of the oversized tunnel to the next set of stairs. Across the stadium-sized dance floor, thousands of club-goers were already gathered, their arms waving together as a collective organism to the increasingly electric trance beat.

Spread throughout the writhing crowd were more than a dozen circular bars, the stainless steel bar tops lined with pyramids of bottled water. One of the bartenders poured a fluid onto a bar top and with a lighter created an instantaneous crescent of fire. This triggered other bartenders to do the same. As Stratos led the group across the catwalk, a cascade of small eruptions of flame burst from the stations across the dance floor. The fountains of flame burning off among the thousand blinking lights reminded Cameron of a chemical facility in full process. He was not far off. The group ascended a metal stairwell. Directly below, in a small sectioned off booth, a shirtless tattooist was inking a young lady's thigh, while next to him another partier reclined back in a barber chair rhythmically rolling her head side to side to the techno beat as a heavily inked bald girl slid an immensely long needle through the upper edge of her belly button.

Another story higher, the stairs opened to a raised platform. An intimate crowd of less than fifty lounged on the sofas, apparently oblivious to anyone not touching them, and a few were involved in some heavy touching. A few people, a bit more coherent, held company near the bar at the wall. A raised silk sheet, glowing peach from behind, lined the end of the platform farthest from the outer dance floor. Cameron imagined the extremes of the touching that was happening behind the privacy veil. The deejay was working some type of voodoo on a raised tier at the end of the platform. Surrounded by an array of small screens and electronic components, the Pied Piper of sorts enchanted, what appeared to Cameron as a mass of protoplasm, with musical mayhem.

Annalisa leaned into Cameron's ear. "He's great, isn't he?"

Cameron could barely hear Annalisa. "Who is he?"

"He calls himself MooreHouse, like more house, get it?"

"Clever," said Cameron.

"During the summer top producers and dance deejays come to the island in between touring and play at Stratosphere. Some of the most famous deejays run their own weekly nights right here. They use Ibiza for presenting new songs."

"Is that so?" asked Cameron, raising his brows.

"You can barely hear me?" asked Annalisa.

Cameron smiled and nodded his head.

Annalisa nodded and gestured for Cameron and Pepe to follow her, and then nodded to Stratos. Stratos returned the nod and headed toward the bar. At the wall past the deejay, Annalisa punched a keypad. The door opened to a small private lounge. The three stepped inside. The lounge was not that much different than a private box at any large stadium, the outer wall a pane of glass overlooking the entirety of Stratosphere. Once inside, Cameron noticed that there were several similar panes surrounding the upper level. The room was furnished with oversized stuffed sofas like those on the outer platform and the necks of champagne protruded from two buckets of ice.

Annalisa closed the door behind them, her voice clear and lowered to a normal level, "Would you be so kind as to pour, Mister Kincaid?"

The noise dissipation of the small lounge had an immediate sobering quality.

Cameron and Pepe each shifted their jaws opened and closed.

"Sorry," said Annalisa. "The room is soundproof," she shirked her shoulders, "also pressurized." Next to the door, Annalisa pressed a button on a small console and the remainder of the music dropped away. Even the incredibly deep thumps of the bass had disappeared.

"That's better," said Annalisa. "Now we can hear ourselves. Should I order something to eat?"

"No," said Pepe. "We should not be here so long."

Annalisa smiled, "Why, of course not. Will you indulge me with champagne, though? I admit I love the bubbles."

Pepe gave Annalisa a gracious smile. "Certainly, where are my manners? Kincaid, let me do the honors." Pepe removed one of the bottles from the ice and began to prepare three glasses.

Annalisa moved to the edge of the sofa. "May we sit, gentlemen?"

"Certainly," said Cameron. "After you."

The lounge was surreal in a way the world outside of the door was not. With the speaker to the sound system adjusted so low, the soundproofing and air system had the effect of sterilizing the environment. When they had first entered the room, Cameron had thought of the huge window as a voyeuristic display into the esoteric world beyond the glass. His perspective was shifting. Sitting with Annalisa on the sofa, he felt, with the long pause silences, that they could be on exhibit.

Cameron's mind raced. Perhaps they were on exhibit. "Will Demetrius be joining us?"

"Shortly, I believe," said Annalisa. She reached for the

champagne Pepe offered and then raised the glass. "I would like to make a toast."

"I will further indulge you," said Pepe. He and Cameron were not aloof to Annalisa stalling and, though they were sympathetic to the beautiful assistant, their mission was not to be subdued.

"To a wonderful evening," said Annalisa.

"Cheers," said Cameron and Pepe.

CHAPTER 65
STRATOSPHERE, IBIZA

Holding her champagne close, Annalisa peered deeply at Cameron. Her eyes burning coals, her hair blown and flowing, Annalisa began to slowly ease the sheer white blouse over her shoulders, in a very nonchalant, purposely seductive action.

Across the table, Pepe's lips tightened. Cameron could almost feel bad for this girl. So obviously put to task.

"Miss Droukos," said Pepe.

Annalisa kept her gaze locked on Cameron. "Annalisa, please," she said.

"Miss Droukos," Pepe repeated. "We have been waiting quite some time. Either Demetrius has found Nikos or he has not. Either way, I believe we are finished here."

"I told you. Mister Stratos will be along shortly. Please share some of this champagne with me. This second bottle is better than the first." Annalisa smiled softly. "You must tell me what it is like to be the famous Dragon Chef." She slid her hand across the cushion in Cameron's direction. "Women love a man that can cook. I bet you get a lot of attention."

Cameron sighed and straightened his back. "I am

sorry. We are here for one reason. I think it's time we speak to Nikos. His father has obviously found him."

Annalisa leaned forward, her breast revealed and almost falling away from the top that held them.

"Unless your next move is to strip off that bikini top and wrap and share your pleasures with us, I assure you, you have run out of game," said Pepe.

Annalisa sat upright. "Mister Laroque—"

"And I should further advise you that in this special instance, even the temptation of fruit such as yours will not restrain our pursuit of Nikos Stratos."

Annalisa went stone-faced for a moment. "Five more minutes, Cameron. Mister Stratos is on his way."

"Why five minutes?" Cameron's eyes flashed wide. "The earpiece. She hears them."

Cameron dashed to the windowpane. Demetrius and Nikos were fleeing to the exit off the edge of the catwalk below.

"We will be leaving now," said Cameron.

"Please, let Mister Stratos handle this and I am sure everything will be fine."

"Get her, the door is locked," said Cameron.

Pepe offered his hand to Annalisa. "May I help you up?"

"Why?" asked Annalisa.

"We need you to get us out of here," said Pepe.

"I suggest you do as he asks, Miss Droukos," said Cameron. "You will be very easy to carry, conscious or unconscious."

Annalisa stood and then finished her champagne in one drink. "They are not going to let you leave."

Cameron flashed his eyes up to Pepe. "I believe we can convince them."

Pepe reached for Annalisa's arm. She defiantly jerked away and went to the console. She tapped a short code. "Stay and there is no trouble."

"I find that is seldom the case," said Cameron. "Stand

back."

At the first crack of the door, the heavy trance beat bass flooded the room. The sense of urgency, the adrenalin, the force that was pushing Cameron, accelerated in intensity. He pulled the door in wide. The light of the lounge must have caught the peripheral of the deejay. Deejay MooreHouse shifted his gaze from his console to Cameron. The deejay held a sunglass stare that looked into and through Cameron, and then with a nod, slid a fader on one of his boards, leveling up a new rapid mix. Cameron returned the nod, unsure what prompted the deejay.

Instantly, Cameron had an answer.

A muscle bound Black Tee, locked onto Cameron, emerged from a dark shadow across the platform. Not to be too obvious to the approaching thug, Cameron relaxed and went into a subtle relaxed Taekwondo attention stance, the Charyeot stance. His body already in an upright standing position, his legs side by side, heels touching, toes slightly apart, Cameron dropped his hands parallel to his body and relaxed, proper to his training. To the arrogant Black Tee, Cameron would appear to be standing in the door waiting unprepared for a confrontation. Cameron was waiting, yet very prepared. Already ultra focused, the techno added a hypersensitivity. Cameron saw a slight acknowledgement in the approaching Black Tee's eyes, not toward Cameron, but to someone to the side of the door. When the second Black Tee spun into the doorframe, Cameron was expecting him. This Tee, a crew cut blonde, held up his flat hand in front of Cameron in a signal that the group should not move. Then in an action of brawn and inexperience the massive Tee smirked at Cameron and made the brutal mistake of shoving his meaty hand forward. The ape must have only seen a blur as Cameron slid to the side, clutched the man lightly by his wrist, and with little effort, used the man's own momentum to send him flying into the lounge. As he flew by Pepe, he received a solid elbow to the base of his skull that sent him crashing to the floor.

Upon seen his cohort disappear behind Cameron, the first Black Tee went rooster, his chest filling with rage and emotion, a critical flaw. The Black Tee raised his arms, his delts, pects, and lats pumped full. Cameron was sure steroids had dumbed down this giant. When the grizzly of a man was close, Cameron surprised the man with a quick Gunnun Sogi stance, a solid step forward followed through with a full on thrust to the Black Tee's breadbasket. The Black Tee's eyes screamed wide and his knees buckled. The tribal pulse of the music bore into Cameron's center. Another Black Tee thundered toward Cameron.

Cameron and Pepe exited the lounge. Pepe met the Black Tee first.

This third Black Tee was thinner, compact, and more agile than the first two. What he lacked in mass, he made up for in skill. Seeing Cameron's style of maneuver, the Tee approached in a Taekwondo fighting stance, rattled off two strikes that Pepe easily repelled and then fluidly went into a back-L stance, one foot on the ground, the other a flying kick toward Pepe's head. The blow may have been fatal had the man not failed at rule number one, know your audience. Pepe of course practiced Taekwondo. Pepe practiced Kung Fu. Pepe practiced Karate. Pepe was a master at Judo. Pepe effortlessly dodged the nimble assailant, his rotund upper body gyrating on his lowered knees, his head slipping back out of the way, his forearm sliding up to gently assist the younger man's leg away. Well trained, the Black Tee used Pepe's assist to thrust him into a spin and as his body curled around, raising his other leg to smash Pepe's ribs, forcing him to the wall. Pepe grimaced, the air crushed from his lungs. He dropped his arm over the young Black Tee's leg and rolled himself hard forward against the wall, splitting the limb out sideways away from the knee, the action and young man's anguish silent beneath the electronic beat, ever increasing to a mind blowing rate.

Everyone else on the platform seemed oblivious to what had happened. No one left for the other room or even sat up. No one appeared to notice, no one except for Annalisa. Outside the entrance to the lounge, Annalisa had lost expression.

"C'mon!" screamed Cameron.

Annalisa did not hear Cameron. He seized her arm, alerting her back from wherever she had checked out to. She turned her still vacant face toward him, and a glint of recognition filled her eyes. Cameron tilted his head toward Pepe and the stairwell and in a normal voice said, "Let's go." He was sure that beneath the volume of the pulsing unearthly music, she could not hear him.

Annalisa nodded and then began to move toward the exit.

CHAPTER 66
STRATOSPHERE, IBIZA

As more of a matter of training than formal protocol, Cameron remained by the door while Pepe led Annalisa down the metal stairs to the catwalk. He mentally divided the VIP level into quadrants and then scanned them one by one in search of anyone that was not subdued by a drug heavy trance or that appeared to be taking too much interest in him. Both he and Pepe had seen cameras hidden among the overhead lights. Regardless of whether the occupants of the VIP level had paid attention to their tussle with security, in a facility this size, someone was watching. Reinforcements were on the way. Confident the level was clear, Cameron twisted, clutched the rails of the stairwell, and slid down. They had almost crossed the catwalk when a Black Tee appeared from the exit, took two strides, and then nimbly sprung forward into a front facing stance. Pepe fluidly dropped into a shallow standing squat, an agile position giving him the flexibility to launch both attacks and defences against the formidable Tee.

The open catwalk was a maelstrom of electronic pulses, bass beats, and a sublime and ethereal swooning female chorus.

Panicked by the appearance of the Black Tee at the exit, Annalisa spun back toward Cameron. Her eyes flashed in horror, alerting him. He ducked and twisted short of an attack from a second Black Tee that had managed to elude him on the VIP platform and shadow them down.

Electric dance music was not something Cameron ever listened to, yet fighting was like dancing, and he was exhilarated.

The bass beat was pounding at a crushing speed. Bright flashes of brilliant color punctuated lightning fast punches. Cameron kept Annalisa in his peripheral. She appeared disoriented, stunned by the rapid strikes and blows, her head switching from one side to the other. Pepe moved uncomfortably close and she almost caught an elbow. She shuffled toward Cameron to a near miss as a foot flew past her face. She sidestepped up and down the catwalk, dodging feet, elbows, and open hands. There was never a need for her concern. Neither Pepe nor Cameron broke a sweat or an expression. The young Black Tees were fluid mechanized warriors. Every move made, whether by Cameron, Pepe, or the two agile security men, was cool and flowing, and occurring at a rate that, especially with the deep trance beat, was incredibly rapid, and remarkably predictable. The maneuvers were textbook, the only moves to make. As was the maneuver that made Annalisa gasp, when in unison, Cameron and Pepe positioned themselves on the far sides of the catwalk fight and their opponents close to her.

Between punches, Cameron caught Annalisa's eyes go wide and bright, and he shot her a devious smile. If she guessed the move was choreographed, she would have been right. Cameron and Pepe had practiced the move for staged bar brawls and the next part was Cameron's favorite. The two gave each other a nod when they were ready, and then each thrust a body blow to their opponent, penetrating to the true solar plexus, the dense cluster of nerve cells located behind the stomach, right below the diaphragm. The blow was intended to cause great pain, knock the wind out of the Black Tees, and most important, the simultaneous action was designed to shove the Tees into each other. The modification was that Annalisa was between them. The move worked. For a split second, the Black Tees' attention was drawn away from their opponents to the overwhelming pain in their gut, and to Annalisa between them. In that opportune slice of time, when the Tees turned toward her, Cameron and Pepe squeezed each by the back of the head, seized them by the crotch, and then flung the Tees airborne over the side of the catwalk.

In that sudden instant, as the two Black Tees arced high above the crowd, the thunderous backbeat that had shaken the building in a constant quake abruptly stopped. Silence, an unworldly hush, descended over the crowd, and then, echoing through the cavernous building in a soft repetitive whisper, "All for you, all for you, all for you—"

Cameron peered out into the hall, into the writhing mass gone calm, and then he looked up at Deejay MooreHouse. Deejay MooreHouse, way too cool in his sunglasses and heavy headphones, was smiling widely at Cameron. The deejay nodded his head, extended his arm, and then pointed his index finger straight to Cameron. "All for you, all for you, all for you—" Cameron smiled up to the deejay and shot his finger back, and then Deejay MooreHouse, in a dramatic motion, swung his arm up and around to jab down on the soundboard. The maelstrom of sound returned tenfold and the crowd of faithful thousands rallied. Deejay MooreHouse nodded at Cameron again, and Cameron returned the gesture.

CHAPTER 67
STRATOSPHERE, IBIZA

The two muscle bound Black Tees waiting at the valet stand were no surprise to Cameron. The calm of the fresh evening air, or maybe the reality shift of stepping out of the club, had subdued him. Cameron felt no need to launch into another confrontation.

Cameron smiled, sucked in a breath, and then said, "Gentlemen, the Aston Martin Rapide please."

The two men appeared uneasy. Their focus slipped past Cameron to Annalisa. "Miss Droukos," one of them said, "we have strict instructions from Mister Stratos that the gentlemen that came with you are to remain here until he returns."

Stepping forward Annalisa sighed, "I am sure you do. However, we are ready to go, so..." She shrugged her brows and reached for the velvet rope.

The second Black Tee found some confidence and moved to block Annalisa. "I'm sorry, Miss Droukos. Mister Stratos was very—" He paused searching for a word.

"Explicit?" offered Annalisa.

"Yes, explicit." He scowled, then said, "You need to go back in the club now."

Pepe put himself between the Black Tee and Annalisa to undo the velvet rope himself. His voice was stern, "I don't think that is going to happen."

The brave Black Tee threw his hand flat up against Pepe's chest and said, "I believe that's exactly what is going to happen."

Pepe slowly tilted his head up from the rope to meet the bouncer eye to eye with a look that let the Black Tee know he had made a mistake.

Annalisa scrunched her nose. Cameron winced an eye near closed, the image of a jet about to collide with a train and knowing that nothing could stop what was about to happen.

The velvet rope was no longer an issue as the bold Black Tee tore the hardware away when Pepe threw him into the driveway. The other bodyguard responded out of a sense of loyalty to his friend and duty to his job, yet only half heartedly, as he did not actually strike a punch at Cameron. He raised his fist into a boxing stance a safe distance away so he would still appear in play. The tossed down Black Tee began to stand. Pepe had taken two strides toward him when, from inside the nightclub, two more Black Tee security guards appeared. These two upped the game, as they each had Taser sticks in hand.

Pepe shook his head. "Really?" Then from the back of his waist he produced his Beretta M9, triggering Cameron to draw his Ruger.

The four Black Tees looked at each other and then the bold one said, "You cannot shoot all of us."

"I cannot believe you just said that," said Cameron.

The four Black Tees shared a glance, and then, bending forward, began to move toward Cameron and Pepe.

Annalisa screamed, "Stop! Stop!"

Everyone looked at Annalisa. They did stop. Right where they stood.

Annalisa spread her hands out, pressing them to the air, and spoke calmly at first, her voice rising as she went on,

"Okay, this is enough. These two men are obviously trained killers. Unless you all want to die, I suggest you prepare the car, and I will smooth things over with Mister Stratos."

The first bold Black Tee eyed Cameron and Pepe thoroughly, then asked, "Trained killers, Miss Droukos?"

Cameron flashed his brow.

"Get the car!" said Annalisa.

"Yes, right now," said the jolted Black Tee. "I'll get the car." He scurried toward the Aston Martin while the other three Black Tees began cleaning up the pieces of their broken velvet rope.

CHAPTER 68
IBIZA

The bi-xenon headlamps sprayed the road to Ibiza Town bright blue, far beyond the flying Aston Martin Rapide.

Pepe tapped his knuckles against the back window. "Can't you make this car go any faster?"

"It's an illusion," said Cameron. "We're moving fine."

"Huh?"

"We're almost to Ibiza Town."

Pepe curled his lip. He pushed his forehead against the glass and peered up through the darkness into the starry sky. In a low voice, he muttered, "Rich or not, who buys an Aston Martin with an automatic transmission."

Cameron flashed his eyes briefly from the road to the rearview, then dropped them back again. "A stick wouldn't move us any faster. Besides, they only make this model in automatic."

Annalisa reached for the stereo. "Mister Stratos is partial to Aston Martins. A close friend once owned the company."

Cameron placed his hand on Annalisa's. "Please, enough music for a little while."

Annalisa pulled her hand back to her lap. Cameron considered her situation. The situation Nikos and his father had put her in.

"Hey," said Cameron. "I thought you told us the garage in Gstaad was full of Lamborghinis and Ferraris. Are you telling me he has close friends in every one of those companies?"

Annalisa lowered her head, a bit embarrassed, and grinned. "You wouldn't believe it but, yes," she raised her head and looked at Cameron, "he does."

"In every one?" said Cameron.

"In every one," said Annalisa. Then they both began to laugh.

Annalisa sighed. "I guess it all sounds kind of ridiculous."

"He is who he is," said Cameron. He let the Aston Martin decelerate. On the road ahead of them, an unmoving line of red taillights trailed toward the glow of Ibiza Town on the near horizon.

"Is there always this much traffic on this little island?" asked Cameron.

Annalisa lifted her head in an attempt to see up and around the cars in queue ahead of them. "After sunset people are finding their way to dinner I guess."

Cameron rested his forearm on the steering wheel. They would have to wait for traffic to begin to move. With the tips of his fingers, he began to tap the top edge of the dashboard, a nervous habit that went with his mind wandering to where he may find Nikos, to where he may find Christine, because with one, would be the other.

Cameron tilted his head to the side and absently peered ahead to the roundabout. "There they are," he said.

"Where?" asked Annalisa. "Where do you see them? How do you know it's them?"

"Up there in the roundabout. The LED in the taillight is out. They didn't get far ahead of us."

Annalisa craned her head closer to Cameron for a clear

view of the roundabout. "I don't see them."

Cameron shifted his fingers on the dashboard to the left. "They took that turnoff. They're not going to the house or airport."

Pepe put his hands on either side of Annalisa's seat and pulled himself forward. "Where are they going, Miss Droukos?"

Annalisa's eyes, fresh a mere moment ago, were dark and tired. Cameron winked at Annalisa, triggering a frail smile in return. "I'd love to drive around all night, but we do need to help a friend."

This time Annalisa was quick to respond, "That turnoff leads to the port. They are going to Mister Stratos' sailing yacht."

"Of course," said Pepe, "that's why there were no signs of Christine. Nikos is hiding her on the yacht."

Cameron gripped the steering wheel and switched his head side to side. Driving forward to maneuver around the queue of cars was not an option. To the right was an iron fence and a boundary of boulders, and to the left was a meter high concrete median. Cameron and Pepe needed to uncomfortably bide their time until they made their way to the roundabout. After an eternal five minutes, they were clear of the median barrier on the left. Cameron gunned the accelerator and the Aston bounced up onto the curb. Dirt, dust, and stones flew up behind the car as Cameron tore through the loose dry sandy soil and shrubbery of the median and into the opposing lane. Circumventing the frozen traffic that had held them, he aimed the Aston toward the roundabout, ignoring any vehicles in his way. A small VW station wagon turned off the roundabout and into the lane, head on with the accelerating Aston. The horn of the oncoming Volkswagen blared as the vehicle swerved to miss the Aston Martin, then stopped abruptly as the car slammed up against an olive tree. Having barely missed crashing into the VW, the Aston entered the roundabout against traffic. The surprise chance of near collision sent the oncoming barrage of brilliant lights veering into rapidly deviating directions.

The Aston Martin had been still, a whirlwind, corrected, and then was again travelling smoothly. Cameron tweaked the rearview mirror to see if traffic in the roundabout was correcting as well. "You can relax now," he said.

"I'm not sure I can," said Annalisa. Her clawed hands were each clutching a part of the interior dearly, one hand the dash, the other the door.

"Which way now?"

"Um, turn right at the next roundabout then go all the way to the end. Mister Stratos keeps the yacht moored in Talamanca Bay."

The cadmium yellow lights that illuminated the white stucco buildings blanketing the hillside Ibiza Town, appeared an anachronism to the flowing headlights that weaved in and out of view. The harbor's forests of masts towering the mammoth powerboats produced the same sense of mixed century.

Cameron slowed as he approached the next roundabout that led down toward the port. The other Aston Martin was far ahead of them, yet in view, skirting the rows of the docked sailboats and cruisers populating the port. Cameron watched Stratos enter the far roundabout and then exit the spoke that led to the second harbor, Talamanca Bay. When Stratos had cleared his view, Cameron killed the lights of the Aston so he could shorten the distance to his quarry in stealth. The plan was good because when Cameron entered the far roundabout, he saw Demetrius and Nikos exiting their sports car at the shoreline parking area, mere meters away. Barely above an idle, the Aston loomed from the spoke onto the side street. The Aston came to rest curbside under the shadow of a tree. Hidden in the darkness, Cameron killed the engine and then decided to slip the key fob into his pocket.

The well-lit parking area, where Demetrius and Nikos

had left their Aston, was intended for those with boats moored out in the bay. From the shadows, Cameron watched the two men walk the length of a long concrete dock past a series of tethered dinghies. Nikos climbed into one of the dinghies near the end of the long dock, followed by his father. Demetrius untied the line and then pushed the boat away from the dock. Cameron watched Nikos tug a few times on the four stroke motor cable. With a purr, the dinghy veered out of the pool of light cast from the dock and into the bay.

A short way out, a number of masts sprouted from the surface of Talamanca Bay. Mooring lines, strung with lamps, appeared to rest on the reflecting amber sheets that shot across the still water from the shoreline hotels.

"Which one?" asked Pepe. His elbow supported him on the center console as he watched the two Greek men motor away.

"Excuse me?" asked Annalisa.

"Which sailboat? They are heading out to one of those boats," said Pepe. "I am guessing one of those three larger yachts."

"The smaller one on the side," said Annalisa.

"I would have guessed one of the larger ones," said Pepe.

"If you think thirty-eight meters is small. Anyway, the size is not what makes the yacht special. The Azulejo is over one hundred years old. Mister Stratos took great pride in restoring and racing the luxury yacht. His son shares the..." Annalisa hesitated, "affection."

Cameron smirked, "Another one of a kind."

"Hmm," said Annalisa.

"Well," said Pepe. "Demetrius and his family did not get to where they are without flaunting a little."

"I told you," said Annalisa. "The Stratos men have the means to obtain what they want, by purchase, or other... Well, they have the means."

"To take what they want," said Cameron

"I am sure they do," said Pepe. "Rather Machiavellian."

"To take what you want?" asked Annalisa.

"Not that," said Pepe. "I am referring to the power a one of a kind item brings to those like Stratos that wish to attain and maintain power."

"How so?"

"There is more to the acquisition of particular items. A key to creating and maintaining power is to create compelling spectacles, full of symbols that heighten presence. Machiavelli said people are always impressed by the superficial appearance of things."

"I may disagree that a century old luxury yacht is superficial."

"Does owning the boat make a difference in the man?"

"Fascinating, Mister Laroque," said Annalisa.

"Yes, fascinating," said Pepe. "There is another fascinating key to maintaining position and power that you appear to know so well."

"What is that?"

"Pose as a friend, work as spy."

"I'm sorry?"

Cameron smiled, "I do believe Stratos is genius for sending you in. You are top notch, short of weapons training. Where did you study?"

"Cambridge, then Harvard Law."

"Huh," Cameron glanced over at Annalisa, her naked flesh beneath the sheer blouse glistening bright in the dim interior of the car. "Brains and beauty," he said. "A slam dunk really."

"I'm not sure I follow," said Annalisa.

"Sure you do," said Cameron.

Annalisa hung her head down for a moment and then, in a soft tone said, "Foreknowledge cannot be elicited from ghosts and spirits, it cannot be inferred from comparison of previous events, or from the calculations of the heavens, but must be obtained from people who have knowledge of the enemy's situation."

"Sun-tzu," said Cameron. "He was right, tough to shoot ducks blindfolded."

Pepe held his hand out between them. "The earpiece please."

CHAPTER 69
TALAMANCA BAY, IBIZA

Even without the motor, the dinghy swiftly glided across the smooth surface of Talamanca Bay. From the dock, the bay had appeared mostly brilliant with the reflection from the lights of the beach hotels and mired with shadow where the light was absent. Out in the midst of the harbor, the above light of hillside Ibiza Town, and the myriad of stars that peppered the sky, made the interior of the small craft as well lit as the shore.

The Azulejo, like the other yachts near her, was lit by the strings of lamps along her moorings and up her masts. Cameron and Pepe saw two other dinghies tied to her stern. One of the dinghies had been brought out to the luxury sailing yacht by Demetrius and Nikos ahead of Cameron and Pepe, the other they surmised may belong to Azulejo. Perhaps Nikos had assigned someone with the task of caring for his captive. The task of feeding and securing Christine, ensuring she not leave the yacht, taking measures she remained below.

Men bickering, peaked with a few hollers, carried across the surface of the water.

Cameron's mind wandered to what he and Pepe would

find inside the cabin. His stomach tightened.

The end of the dinghy's towline was looped and ready. Pepe snagged a cleat at the stern. Cameron palmed some resistance to the warm hull as Pepe softly pulled the small craft tight to the yacht. No one was on deck. Light escaped from the open cabin.

The occupants of the yacht no longer quarreled loudly. The discussion ensued, muffled below within the hull.

Weapons drawn, Pepe and Cameron eased themselves onto the deck of the Azulejo.

Hunched over and incredibly nimble for the added girth of his age, Pepe scurried toward the foredeck hatch, the most likely place to find his sister. Cameron remained aft and waited until his partner was in position. From around the mast he could see Pepe lift the forward hatch.

His head focused below deck, Pepe threw Cameron a hand signal to signify he thought the forward cabin was clear. That was good and bad. The signal also meant Pepe did not see Christine. Then Pepe slipped into the yacht.

Huddling next to the main cabin door, Cameron began a slow count to five to allow Pepe to work his way aft. Though the forward cabin may be empty, Cameron was certain that at least Demetrius and Nikos were beyond the open hatch in front of him. There was also someone else with them. Cameron was close enough to make out the discussion. Someone was speaking with a British accent.

An accent Cameron immediately recognized. He knew the owner of the third dinghy well.

On the count of five, Ruger in hand, Cameron swung around and into the main cabin. Pepe pushed open the opposite door. Between Cameron and Pepe was Demetrius and Nikos. Signaled by the earpiece Demetrius took their entry in stride, while Nikos, having seen the two men kill firsthand, twitched his head uncomfortably side to side. On the side berth, in front of the Greeks, half awake, drugged, Pepe's sister Christine. Sitting on the berth next to Christine, one leg casually crossed over the other, his arm protectively wrapped around her, and his Walther PPK pointed at the father and son, was the yellow haired Alastair Main.

CHAPTER 70
TALAMANCA BAY, IBIZA

That Pepe had not shot every breathing being upon entering the cabin, besides Cameron and Christine, was a marvel. Cameron had his Ruger drawn in the general direction of father and son. Pepe had his Beretta raised to Nikos' head. Key to the two of them was that Alastair had his PPK pointed at the mogul and his scion, though neither Cameron or Pepe wanted to decipher Alastair's reason or intent. Unwanted doubt eased its way into their heads, memories of a past life flooding them with confusion. Not merely any other man, Alastair Main was brother-in-arms to Cameron and Pepe, more than that, a real brother, as tight as blood. The man was a Green Dragon of the highest honor. For an unfathomable number of missions Alastair, an unquestionable shot with camera or rifle, had been the unseen back up, hidden in a van or high on a perch. Alastair had saved Cameron's life on countless missions.

Neither Demetrius nor Nikos immediately spoke. Neither appeared dumbfounded, though Cameron calculated a safe bet would be that the two were not accustomed to having guns pointed at them, let alone three.

Cameron opted to size up what he and Pepe had

walked into. They were leaving with Christine in a matter of minutes regardless, and if Pepe lost patience and began to drop wealthy Greeks, well, that would have to happen. Cameron smirked in the most devious fashion. "Good evening, gentlemen," he said. "Sorry we were late. Did we miss anything?"

Pepe pressed his Beretta to Nikos temple. "We must be missing something."

"I had planned on having this wrapped up before you arrived," said Alastair. "Then again, I expected you a bit sooner, so I suppose the delay is mine."

A proper response from Alastair, a good sign.

Pepe grunted, "Cameron has spent too much time with Americans, always late."

Cameron whimsically raised a brow. "We were detained."

Apparently made confident by the banter, Demetrius spoke up, "And where is my lovely assistant?"

Pepe chuckled, "Miss Droukos is in the trunk of the Aston Martin."

"She's safe," said Cameron. "Pillow, blanket. We didn't want any interruptions, you understand."

Demetrius nodded his head, and then said, "I understand."

"I heard part of a..." Cameron paused flashing his eyes between Nikos and Alastair, "*discussion* when we arrived. Do continue."

Alastair raised his chin. "Mister Stratos was just asking Nikos to explain himself."

"Yes, gentleman," said Demetrius. He pressed his hands down into the air to express his case. "I assure you that I do not condone whatever has led to Miss Laroque residing on this yacht in—" he hesitated, "whatever condition she is in." He shifted his attention to Nikos. "Can you please explain to everyone what is going on."

Pepe pulled the Berretta a small bit away from Nikos' temple and then jabbed the barrel back against him with enough force to cause the playboy to shuffle. "Yes, please Nikos," said Pepe. "Explain to everyone what is going on."

Demetrius' eyes flared contemptuously at Pepe.

A spoiled man-child always told yes, and never maliciously assaulted, Nikos cheeks flushed at Pepe's blunt strike to his temple. His contempt, however, appeared to be directed at his father. Nikos acknowledged Pepe, his mouth tight across his face, leered at his father, and then he began to lash out. Tossing away the feint persona of the playful jetsetter, his tone became defiant and full of disgust, "You never believed I could set up my own deals. I wanted to show you I could."

Demetrius shook his head. "What are you talking about?" he asked. "That thug Dada had several contracts with me. He has done work for me and everyone else. You merely tried to broker a contract that was already set with Abbo."

"I wanted something more than that." Nikos' lip curled to a snarl. "Everything is you, you, you. I wanted to set up a future for myself. My empire."

"That is ridiculous." Demetrius held up a finger. "One day, everything that is mine will become yours."

Nikos raised his voice, "No. I wanted something that was mine. I found out from Feizel the deal you had with the National Volunteer Coast Guard. He bragged about the deal. For five euros a ton, his father allowed you to dump millions of tons of hazardous waste into Somali water. The fool thought his father was a genius. I know better. You charge one thousand euros a ton across Europe, pay the fool a fraction, and then pocket the difference. I made a better deal with Ibrahim Dada."

Demetrius frowned, "You found another fool."

Nikos scowled, "I figured if I could take Abbo out of the mix and get Dada the deal, he would cut me in, and I was right. We agreed he would charge ten euros a ton and give me three. He was happy to make the deal. He already had almost all of the arranged hijacking contracts. He was already going after control of Abbo's gun trade in Dubai, and with control of the waste and fisheries, he would have everything."

"You're heir to a billionaire," said Cameron. "Why bother for a few million euros?"

Alastair frowned, "All of this trouble because of daddy issues."

Pepe shook his head, "He wanted to prove he could undermine the old man."

Demetrius gazed at Nikos in disbelief. "You are my son," he said. "Why would you do this?"

"To show you I could," said Nikos. "Hijacking the Kalinihta was easy to pin on Abbo. Feizel was on board from the start. I convinced him we were the new generation, the next regime. He ate that up."

"You are the next generation," said Demetrius.

"Yes, but like me, Feizel did not want to wait for his father to die to take his turn. He wanted to show his father that he was capable of doing more in their clan. Dada provided the men to take the Kalinihta, and the Somali Marines had taken the compound north of Kismayu from the Merca Group, close enough to call the place Abbo's. Feizel loved the plan. My old buddy Feizel was partying with me all the way from the Seychelles to the compound. Dada even supplied the additional explosives to level the place when we left. Bit overkill, I admit. I thought the over the top explosions would be the give away."

Cameron was puzzled. "Feizel had a gun pointed at you."

"Yes, he thought that was part of the plan, and well, it was. I put an unloaded gun in his hands and told him we would be safe if he pointed it at me," said Nikos. "He was so high he would have done whatever I told him."

Pepe stared stone-faced at Nikos, and then said, "He kept waving the gun back and forth."

"My .50 caliber Desert Eagle is gold-plated, very heavy, and I don't think he'd ever held a gun before," said Nikos.

"He did not even know the thing was Israeli or he probably would not have touched it. The only part of my plan that was missing was how to safely get myself out of there without anyone finding too much out." Nikos leered at his father. "Your people may have been too thorough."

Alastair shook his head. "And that's where I came in."

Nikos nodded at Alastair. "Alastair had been my safari guide in Kenya, and I had gotten to know him. I knew he had once been a commando. I invited him to ski in Gstaad where he blended right in. Did you fellows know your friend here is descended from the peerage? His real name is not even Main, that's his middle name. His real name is Alastair Main Bulteel-Boyd." Nikos winked at Alastair. "You didn't think I knew. Bulteel-Boyd in the SAS before the GCP and then off the radar for a while. I did a background check, of course. That's how I found out we both knew Christine and then, more importantly." Nikos tilted his head back toward Pepe. "I accidently make the connection of how he knew Christine; he saw a photo of me with my arm around her, and recognized her right away. I remember he told me that if anything ever happened to Christine, there would be a string of commandos at the door." Nikos held his hands up in the air. "And then like magic, everything came together. And he was right, you two flew into the rescue with no questions asked."

Pepe swung his Berretta over toward Alastair's face. His already red eyes glazing, "You did this for money."

Alastair held his hand up in defense toward Pepe. "Whoa! Whoa! He played me the same as you. I thought we would find her in Dubai. When Abbo mentioned Dada I suspected a double-cross and tracked Nikos here."

Demetrius grabbed his son's shoulder. "Why do you have the girl?" he asked.

"At the compound, everything was falling into place. Dada's man Tijon, the bald giant, had shown me the exhilaration of pain when I let him beat me. The adrenalin mixed with the cocaine Feizel and I did back at the compound helped me see my—" Nikos pursed his lips, "—invincibility. I knew I could finally begin to make things really happen, to shape things the way I wanted them to be. I had manipulated you, Abbo, Dada, Feizel, Alastair, everybody. I never felt so in control with so much power, a puppet master. I told Christine that soon I was going to be making changes when we were free–she of course believed we were prisoners. Anyway, I told her I was going to change my life and I wanted her with me, by my side." Nikos tossed his hands in the air. "She laughed at me, can you believe that? At me? She told me I had been doing too many drugs with Feizel. So I took her."

"So you took her?" asked Pepe.

"To teach her a lesson. To show her I could own her like anything else. I don't know. I did not think everything through. I flew her to the boat in Monaco and have kept her out of it until I could figure everything out."

"What is she on?" asked Pepe.

"Only tranquilizers, nothing more. I figured once she woke up and realized she had to stay with me, everything would work out."

CHAPTER 71
TALAMANCA BAY, IBIZA

Talamanca Bay was far cooler by comparison to the inland climes of Ibiza. With six adults occupying the Azulejo's main cabin, the small space was becoming quite warm. The fury of Demetrius Stratos and Pepe Laroque was increasing the temperature of the cabin several degrees. Both men were angry with Nikos, each for their own reason, yet the nature was the same. Nikos was disloyal and had betrayed the trust of those around him. Demetrius was angered by his son's disloyalty to him and Pepe was angered by Nikos' betrayal to Christine. Nikos was separated from reality, delusional. An heir to thousands of millions, he had created a deception within deceptions to suit unnecessary petty needs, manipulating some and sacrificing others indiscriminately.

Demetrius took in a deep nasal breath. "Take her out of here," he said to the three gunmen. "This needs to end now." He shifted his conversation between the three former Legionnaires. Each of them still held a weapon, all aimed in his general direction. "I did not want to believe you." He pressed his lips tightly together. "I have already set aside an account for you…" he paused, "for your trouble." Demetrius flashed his eyes toward Christine, half conscious on Alastair's shoulder. "There is an exceptional amount set aside for Miss Laroque."

Cameron did not take Demetrius' statements as an offer to lower his weapon, nor did Alastair or Pepe. The tone in which the Greek spoke was not at all convincing. The three knew better.

To confirm Cameron's foreshadowing, Demetrius turned to him, and then slipped his hand under the bottom of his linen shirt. Cameron extended his neck and slightly raised his Ruger.

"Relax," said Demetrius. From the waist of his linen pants Demetrius retrieved an item familiar to Cameron. He held the piece of metal harmlessly across his open palm. Cameron's eyes went wide as did Pepe's. "Back in Gstaad you were admiring my collection," said Demetrius. "I know you know what this is."

Alastair craned his neck. "What do you have?" he asked. "A knife?"

"A dagger," said Pepe.

Cameron frowned, "A Rex Mundi dagger to be more specific."

"What is a Rex Mundi dagger?" asked Alastair. "May I have a look?"

Cameron glanced at Alastair, then back into the eyes of Demetrius. "Rex Mundi, King of the World," said Cameron.

"King of the what?" asked Alastair.

Cameron's brow furrowed. "A terrorist group Pepe and I stumbled upon up in Canada."

Pepe added, "More like a secret cult. They carry these daggers. Cameron and I have quite a collection."

Cameron stepped back from the Greek. "The Rex Mundi operatives we encountered were soldiers. The person that told us about the Rex Mundi implied the people running the show were quite well off."

Demetrius smiled and nodded. "Your friend was quite

correct," he said. "Then again, she is well versed in our ways."

Cameron noted the word 'is' and that meant that the Rex Mundi had never tracked down Nicole, and that they were unaware of what had happened to Marie. They were unaware that Marie had died in the cabin on Lake Ontario, a victim of the Rex Mundi's pursuit. To realize that Demetrius Stratos was part of the twisted clandestine organization that had relentlessly pursued him and the two innocent women of faith he had escorted from New York to Canada, wretched his stomach.

As if looking into Cameron's mind, Demetrius said, "The cell put into action was very sloppy." Demetrius shifted his body back toward the center of the cabin and at the same time, he twirled the dagger from his palm, toward his other hand, so that an index finger was on each end, and then he began to playfully roll the knife in concentric circles, appearing to amuse himself while he spoke. "Ironic that I now owe you a total of three counts of gratitude, Mister Kincaid."

"Yes, ironic," said Cameron.

"You saved my son." Demetrius flashed his eyes at Nikos, then back to his dagger. "Well, you and I both *thought* you saved him. Just the same. And you alerted me to this, shall we say, situation. The greatest thanks I bear is for the extermination of that cockroach Dada." He locked his eyes onto Pepe. "More accordingly, I should thank you."

In a challenge to himself, Demetrius began to spin the dagger more rapidly.

"Dada, you see, was not long for power anyway, a mere pawn. Worse, Dada resisted the true powers that be, colluding with my own son." Demetrius shook his head, "tsk, tsk, tsk."

Demetrius simultaneously straightened his neck and stopped the rotation of the dagger. "Things are in place for a reason." Reduced to a toy, he clutched the dagger by the hilt, yet held the knife away from himself, inspecting the ornament and design. The object appeared foreign to him. "You know my family, during and before World War II, were Nazi collaborators." He met eyes with Cameron and nodded his head. "Really, we were." He then turned to Alastair. "Immediately after the war, we allied with the British. Before all of that, we collaborated with the Turks, and the Brits again before that, always a grander plan spinning the wheel." He moved the hand holding the dagger in a broad circle to illustrate.

Demetrius stopped for an elaborate pause, the attention of the four other men in the room drawn to the hovering metal blade, drawn to him.

"Look, we need these people, people like Dada and Abbo, to serve a purpose. We create them by employing them to service a need. To transfer commodities under the guise of a hijacking, to fulfill insurance contracts that finance new fleets, mercenaries to eliminate non-players. Hell, the Chinese need a place to send the floating fish factory ships that feed their masses. Food, after all, means power. All these and other tasks need to be performed."

"Like dumping toxic waste in the open sea," said Pepe.

Demetrius absently nodded at Pepe. "Those men like Dada and Abbo are minions of a market, men that people like myself created. One might say—" Demetrius paused again. He glared into the shine of the metal blade he held out before him. "One might say, as the Texans are the Arabs, we are the real Somali pirates."

CHAPTER 72
TALAMANCA BAY, IBIZA

Demetrius was certainly convinced of everything he
told those aboard the Azulejo. Demetrius held a Rex Mundi
dagger, yet nothing that he said sounded anything like the
fervor Cameron had heard from the Rex Mundi operative in
Quebec. The way Cameron heard Demetrius, maintaining
power and rank was justified by any means. Then again,
Cameron was well aware that leaders are motivated by a
different agenda than the many parts of an organization.
Cameron himself had been a cog in a wheel when he was a
super commando, never questioning, never daring to
question. That same sense of honor had been used against
him these last days, once again making him a cog in a wheel.

Cameron found himself angry. An anger he decided
was justified. Nikos was the twisted arrogant son of a
billionaire. But Cameron figured Nikos had done too much
ecstasy and cocaine, or plainly was never rooted in reality.
The audacity of this pretty boy to say outright that he took
Christine to teach her a lesson, that he could own her.

Cameron's disdain for Nikos was great, yet it was no
measure to Pepe's. Cameron could read Pepe easily from
where he stood across the cabin. Pepe's own sanity had

been drawn and tested by this ordeal, and there was not much left keeping Pepe's finger from squeezing the trigger of the Berretta angled less than a muzzle flash from Nikos' skull.

Cameron shot his eyes to Alastair. Alastair was a fun loving man, easygoing by nature, a natural calm. To befriend Alastair was to gain a lifelong unquestioned loyalty. The back of Cameron's throat went acidic. The man that had saved his life more times than he knew—literally more times than he knew—had eyes fixed on Nikos no differently than a predator. That is what the betrayal meant.

Yet the playboy's father appeared far more furious with Nikos than the three former Legionnaires. His grandstanding finished, Demetrius gave the hilt of the raised dagger a tighter squeeze. Whether he was punctuating his the end of his speech, or beginning another, Cameron was unsure. Demetrius dropped the hand holding the dagger by his side and then turned to Nikos. He shook his head in short scolding turns. "Tsk, tsk, tsk. You are a naughty one, Nikos."

Cameron tilted his head to the side in disbelief. The father spoke to his grown son as to a three year old. No wonder Nikos was a mess.

Demetrius raised the dagger and began shaking the pointy end to Nikos face. "What would your mother say? You would break her heart. You break my heart. You try to negotiate around me, you deceive your friend Alastair, you double-cross Abbo, Feizel, and then you killed Feizel." Demetrius slipped the dagger into the pocket of his linen pants and then shoved Nikos back. Nikos cowered from his father. "You should know better, Nikos."

Demetrius stepped back from Nikos. He raised his hands in the air. Then Demetrius violently shoved his free hand under Nikos' shirt, into his waist. Nikos pushed at his father's hands. Demetrius slapped him across the face.

Demetrius held his index finger up to Nikos, glared at him sternly, and then he defiantly reached back to Nikos' waist and retrieved a small Ruger. He tossed the gun back and forth in his hands. "What is this?" he asked. "You carry a gun now, too."

Demetrius turned away from Nikos to address all the three Legionnaires. His head floated back and forth across all three as he spoke, "I am sure you are wondering why I so openly shared with you my involvement, my family's involvement, with the Rex Mundi, our relationship clandestine all of these years. They want me to apologize for my son." Demetrius shrugged. "What is a father to do? I have to apologize for my son, and there is only one way to make amends for the damage he has done. There is only one set of terms the Rex Mundi accepts for what he has done. They want me to kill him, of course, and if he were anyone else—" he twirled the barrel of the Ruger toward the ceiling. "Well, I have to spare my son."

Then Demetrius abruptly lowered the Ruger toward Alastair and fired.

Cameron released two rounds into Demetrius' side while Alastair simultaneously fired into his forehead, implanting fragments of the Greek's skull into the hull, killing him instantly.

What may have been a war cry began to escape from Nikos throat as he threw his body forward to charge Cameron. The cry became a gurgle as Pepe's blade clotheslined Nikos, slicing halfway through his neck. Cameron had seen Pepe do this before. The Berretta against Nikos skull had been a prop, the obvious weapon. Pepe had wanted to take Nikos' life with his hands.

Alastair sent a shot from the PPK into Nikos as well, though the partial decapitation was what killed him.

Alastair inspected his shoulders and then the hull around him. "Bloody hell, he missed me."

"He didn't miss," said Cameron. "He was in a corner. He said himself he had to spare his son. He knew we wouldn't. I think his heart was broken. He didn't want to see Nikos die."

"And what was with all of that rambling," said Alastair.

"Demetrius knew he wasn't leaving." Cameron knelt down and took the Rex Mundi dagger from Demetrius' pocket, far more ornamented than the others he had seen, this one had a crimson ruby set in the hilt. Cameron inspected the familiar ruby closely and then lifted Demetrius' hand. The ruby set into his ring was the same cut and size and was encircled with the exact design as the dagger.

"And what about that thing?" asked Alastair. He shifted to allow Pepe to exam Christine's pupils.

"Same thing," said Cameron. "He felt the need to let me know. They know who I am."

"They?" asked Alastair. "Who the bloody hell are they?"

"The Rex Mundi."

"Right."

"I'll fill you in after we get out of here." Cameron nodded toward Christine, her hair mussed, gaze dazed. "She's waited long enough for us." His face froze for a second, "And there is another woman waiting for us to rescue her from the trunk of the Aston Martin."

Alastair peered at Cameron, "We don't have to—,"

Cameron shook his head. "No, she won't talk." He glanced down at Nikos. "Besides, there has been enough unnecessary carnage." Cameron rested his hands, one with a Ruger, the other with the dagger, on his knees and sighed. "Listen, I'm gonna do a wipe down. Let's get her out of here."

Alastair eased Christine upright. "Christine, we need to go."

"Let me help you," said Pepe, slipping his arm beneath his sister. "The anesthetic effect of the drugs will wear off eventually, for now I don't believe she knows what has happened."

~*~

THE END

CAMERON KINCAID RETURNS IN
TEMPLAR FORCE

~*~

ABOUT THE AUTHOR

Daniel Arthur Smith is the author of the international bestsellers *THE CATHARI TREASURE, THE SOMALI DECEPTION,* and a few other novels and short stories.

He was raised in Michigan and graduated from Western Michigan University where he studied meta-physics, cognitive science, philosophy, and comparative religion. He began his career as a bartender, barista, poetry house proprietor, teacher and then became a technologist and futurist for the Fortune 100 across the Americas and Europe.

Daniel has traveled to over 300 cities in 22 countries, residing in Los Angeles, Kalamazoo, Prague, Crete, and now writes in Manhattan where he lives with his wife and young sons.

For more information, visit **danielarthursmith.com**

STAY IN THE LOOP

Following your favorite authors on Facebook, Twitter, or other social media has become a sketchy business. Facebook and other companies block authors from conversing regularly with readers unless they are willing to cough up BIG BUX to 'promote' every post. To make sure you are receiving the latest updates, freebies, and stories on everything in the Daniel Arthur Smith universe you have to join his email newsletter. As a subscriber, you'll receive early Advance Review Copies (ARCS) of all of Daniel's books and stories… for free! In addition to all of that, Daniel regularly gives away lots of other loot like signed books and posters, so make certain that you are subscribed.